Max Runs Away

Danielle Steel
Max Runs Away

Illustrated by Jacqueline Rogers

Delacorte Press

Published by
Delacorte Press
Bantam Doubleday Dell Publishing Group, Inc.
666 Fifth Avenue
New York, New York 10103

Library of Congress Cataloging in Publication Data

Steel, Danielle.
    Max runs away / Danielle Steel ; illustrated by Jacqueline Rogers.
        p.   cm.
    Summary: Jealous of the time his parents spend with his baby
brother and sister, seven-year-old Max leaves home but soon learns
the dangers of running away.
    ISBN 0-385-30213-4
    [1. Runaways—Fiction.   2. Brothers and sisters—Fiction.
3. Safety—Fiction.] I. Rogers, Jacqueline, ill. II. Title.
PZ7.S8143Maxg 1991
[E]—dc20   89-77984
                                          CIP AC

Designed by Judith Neuman-Cantor

Manufactured in the United States of America

November 1990

10 9 8 7 6 5 4 3 2 1

RAN

To Nicky,

*With all my heart and all my
love . . . for all that you are,
and will become . . . for the boy
I have always been so proud of
. . . and always, always will be!
With all my love,*

Mommy

This is Max. He lives in New York, and he is seven years old. His Mommy is a nurse, and his Daddy is a fireman. His Mommy works in a hospital, in the nursery, with the newborn babies. She only works there some of the time now, to help out, because when Max was five, his brother and sister were born. Max's brother and sister are twins, and their names are Charlie—Charlotte for real—and Sam, and they are two years old.

Everyone says they're really cute, and they are, but sometimes Max thinks they're a real nuisance.

Max likes to play with them with his friends, or give them a bath, or push their stroller when they go to the park.

But sometimes he likes them to leave him alone, too, so he can play by himself in his room, or be with his friends without being bothered, or just talk to his Dad without being interrupted.

Sometimes it seems like everything was easier before the twins came along. No one ever played with his toys, or messed up his things, or wanted his Mom when he really needed her. Now it seems as if she's busy all the time chasing after Charlie and Sam, before they hurt themselves or get into too much trouble.

It's not just his Mom. His Dad is busy with them too. In fact, sometimes it seems to Max that no one has any time for him at all.

One day when Max was at school, the teacher
scolded him for not paying attention during their
reading class. But he had been trying to say
something important to his friend. And then at
recess, a little girl with bright red hair teased
him and took his ball away. She almost made
him cry.

At lunchtime he spilled hot chocolate all over his new jeans.

When Jean, his baby-sitter, picked him up she forgot the special treat she had promised to bring him. She was going to bake chocolate chip cookies especially for him. But she said she'd been too busy and hadn't had time to do it. It seemed like nothing went right that day. He'd been hoping his Mom would pick him up, but she couldn't because she was busy with the twins.

When he got home, Max went to his room and
saw what the twins had done that day. They had
taken great big fat crayons, a red one and a
black one and a really yucky green one, and
drawn all over his room. They'd drawn on the
walls and the bedspread and the floor and all
over his favorite pictures that he'd brought home
from school. They'd even drawn on George, the
teddy bear that he liked to sleep with at night.
They had drawn on everything. His Mommy had

tried to clean it up, but the crayon marks just wouldn't come off.

His Mommy told him how sorry she was and that she'd try to clean it up some more when she had time, but he knew she never would. She never had time for anything anymore. Just for the twins. She was always feeding or washing them, or ironing their clothes, or keeping them out of trouble, and when his Dad came home, she needed him to help her too. Max loved the twins too, but lately it just seemed as if no one had any time for him.

And on this particular day, seeing the mess the twins had made in his room just seemed like too much to take for another minute. They had even broken his fire truck, and the ladder was lying next to it on the floor. Just seeing it there made Max angry.

Max sat and looked at the broken fire truck for a long time, and then he quietly closed the door to his room. He was just going to sit and think for a while about the way things used to be. He made up his mind to tell his Dad when he got home about the mess the twins had made. But when Dad got home from the firehouse that night, he fell asleep before Max could even talk to him. He'd been fighting a fire in a warehouse on the Lower East Side. No one was hurt, but it had been a lot of work, and Max's Mommy told him not to disturb his Daddy.

The next morning, when Max got up, things seemed better again for a little while. Sam and Charlie looked really cute at breakfast, and they laughed at all the funny faces Max made at them. His Mom had made his favorite pancakes. She was going to work at the hospital that day, and the twins were going to stay with Jean. It was a beautiful sunny day when Max's Dad dropped him off at school on his way to the firehouse. And Max was happy all day.

His Mom picked him up after school, and then they went to pick up the twins at Jean's. Max couldn't believe his eyes when he got there. The twins had taken George, his favorite teddy bear, to the baby-sitter's. His arm had been torn off, and they'd gotten blue paint on his tail. Max wanted to cry just looking at him.

"Why did you let them take George to Jean's?" Max asked his Mom with eyes full of tears.

"I didn't know they'd taken him," she told him honestly. "You know I wouldn't have let them take him. Sam must have put him in with his own things." Max's Mommy always packed a bag of clothes and toys for them whenever they went to stay at Jean's house. "I'm sorry, sweetheart. I'll fix George tonight, I promise!" She tried to put an arm around Max, but he didn't even want to be close to her, he was so unhappy. It seemed like in the past few months everything was always more difficult because of the twins. They were getting into everything and taking up everyone's time and attention. His Dad said they were going through the terrible twos and they'd settle down eventually, but Max just didn't believe it. He was beginning to think that they were always going to mess up his things and take up all of everyone's attention.

Max went home with his Mom and the twins,
and he was looking very glum. After dinner he
went to his room and played with his fire truck,
even though the ladder was broken. He put
George, his teddy bear, carefully on his bed.
Jean had fastened the arm back on with safety
pins, and his Mom had promised that as soon as
the twins were asleep she would sew it. She was
sure she could get the blue paint spot off too.

But she never got time to take care of George. The twins came down with the flu and she was up all night taking care of them. His Dad wasn't due back from the firehouse until the morning.

And then when he came home he was too exhausted to talk to any of them. Max's Mom was in a hurry when she dropped Max off at school, because there'd been an emergency at the hospital, and she was on her way in to help. Max's Dad had to take care of the twins all day, and he said, as Max and his Mommy went out the door, that he was so tired he didn't see how he was going to do it.

Max knew as he started to walk into the school that today was going to be the same thing all over again when he got home. His Mom and Dad would be tired from work and taking care of the twins. No one would remember to fix his fire truck or sew George's arm on. Mom and Dad said he was a big boy now and he had to understand these things, but it didn't seem like much fun to him. He missed the old days before the twins were born, or even a few months ago, when they were too little to hurt or break anything. Right now, they seemed like too much trouble for everyone, especially Max, who decided he'd just about had it.

That morning, as Max started to walk into school, he stopped and thought about all his problems. His Mom and Dad were too busy with Sam and Charlie. The twins were a pain in the neck. And it seemed to him that nobody really cared what happened to him anymore. They were always busy with Sam and Charlie. Without saying a word, Max walked back out the front door of school after his Mom was gone and ran right around the corner. He was going to run away and start a new life without all these problems.

He stood in the sunshine for a minute,
wondering what to do next and where to go, and
he wasn't really sure. He could go home, but his
Daddy was there and he would wonder why Max
wasn't in school. And he'd be angry at him for
leaving school without a grown-up, because he
always told Max how dangerous it was to go
anywhere without a grown-up with you. He
could go to Jean's, the baby-sitter. She lived only
two blocks away, but she'd be surprised to see
him too, and she would probably scold him. He
could run back around the corner and go back
into school. But it was late, and he'd have to
explain to the teachers where he'd been.

All of a sudden Max realized he couldn't go
anywhere. And if he did, he would be in a lot of
trouble. Without meaning to—or maybe just
meaning to a little bit—he had run away, and
now he wasn't sure what to do about it.

Max was really scared as he stood all by
himself around the corner. He didn't know what
to do or where to go, or if he could ever go home
again, and if he did, how to explain it. He wasn't
sure he could tell anyone how mad he had been
at his Mom and Dad and the twins, or just why.
And as he thought about it now, it all seemed kind
of silly and all he felt was scared and really sorry.

The twins weren't really so bad after all, Max thought as he stood there. They were kind of cute most of the time, even if they were pests and they did get into everything, but he really kind of loved them. He liked bragging about them to his friends and talking about the cute things they had done. And when they were first born, he had even taken them to show-and-tell at school with his Mommy.

And now, maybe he'd never see them, or his Mom and Dad, again. As he thought about it, tears filled his eyes, and two great big tears started to roll down his cheeks. He hadn't brought his teddy bear with him, and he didn't know where to go, so he just started walking. He got all the way to the corner of the next block, but he didn't cross the street, because he wasn't quite sure how to do it. Cars were coming around the corner very fast, and people were hurrying by. New York is a very busy city. Finally, the next time the light turned green, he started to walk across the street all by himself. When a car honked at him, he jumped and ran to the other side of the street.

"And just what are you up to, young man?" a policeman with a big mustache asked him as he reached the sidewalk. "Where are you going all by yourself on this Tuesday morning?"

"I . . . I'm going to school," Max said. He wondered if the policeman would put him in jail if he knew he'd run away from school. Then he remembered his Daddy telling him that policemen were his friends. He knew this policeman was, too, even if he did look a little scary.

"Are you going to school all by yourself?" the policeman asked. Max nodded. "And what school would that be?"

Max told him. And the policeman frowned, looking puzzled.

"Aren't you going the wrong way? Why don't I walk you to school, and make sure that you get there safely?" He smiled at Max. Max felt safe when the big policeman took his hand and they crossed the street again. This time none of the cars honked at him. They all waited very politely for them to cross. "Why were you walking away from school, young man, and not toward it?" he asked with a raised eyebrow. Max didn't say anything, he just looked worried.

And a few minutes later, they were standing in
front of the door of his school. The policeman
rang the doorbell, because the door was locked
since school had already started. A teacher
came to open the door a moment later, and she
was startled to see Max standing next to the
policeman.

"Max . . . I thought you were upstairs by now," she said with a worried look, but just as she looked at him, Max's teacher came hurrying out of her classroom.

"Max . . . where have you been? We've been looking for you everywhere for the last ten minutes." He hadn't been gone for very long, and they weren't even sure he had been out of the building. And no one had realized that he had actually run away from school, even if it was for only a few minutes.

Tears filled his eyes as Max looked at all of them, and he started to cry. It had been scary being out alone on the street, and not knowing where to go, or why he had really done it. "I'm sorry," Max cried. "I was mad at the twins and . . ." The whole story came tumbling out, about the broken ladder on his fire truck, and the paint on George's tail, and the crayon on the wall, and the twins having the flu so his Mommy couldn't sew up George's arm. It all sounded jumbled and silly, but to Max it was very important. The police officer smiled down at him, and the teacher said she understood how he felt.

She sat down and put him on her lap as they talked, and she reminded him of how dangerous it was to go out in the street without a grown-up.

"I know," he said, tears still rolling down his cheeks. None of it seemed as important anymore, or as terrible. In fact, he wished he were at home with his Mommy and Daddy and the twins. He never wanted to run away again. It had been a silly thing to do and he knew it.

The policeman left, and the teacher called
Max's Daddy. And he came to see Max with the
twins in the stroller. They were feeling better by
then, and his Daddy looked very serious as he
sat down next to Max. They talked about what
had happened, while one of the assistant
teachers kept Sam and Charlie busy.

"I just thought you and Mommy were busy with the twins all the time. No one ever pays any attention to me anymore. Everyone's always talking about them, and they break all my things . . ." But his Dad already knew. He had sewed George's arm back on while the twins took their nap that morning. And he had gotten the blue paint off George's tail with a little bit of paint remover. George was as good as new, he told Max, and Max blew his nose and smiled at his Daddy.

"And I fixed your ladder truck too. It's all fixed now." His Dad smiled at him. He loved Max more than Max had ever realized, and so did Max's Mommy. Max snuggled close to him, feeling safe and loved and happy. "I want you to finish the day at school now, and I'll come back to pick you up later." Then his Daddy looked serious again. "Running away was the wrong thing to do, Max, and something really frightening could have happened. You could have gotten lost or taken away by someone you don't know. Or hurt. Running away is no way to solve a problem."

"I know that, Dad," Max said solemnly. "I was really scared once I did it. I didn't know what to do after I left school and walked around the corner."

"Don't you *ever* do that again. If you do, you'll be punished. But maybe this time it was a good lesson." His Dad held him tight for a long moment, while Max thought how glad he was to have such a terrific Daddy. And when Max went back to his classroom the twins waved to him.

Later, his Daddy picked him up after school,
and he came alone. He had left the twins at
home with Max's Mommy. Max walked slowly
home with him, glad that he was going home and
that nothing terrible had happened to him that
morning.

At home, Max's Mommy and the twins were waiting for them. The door to Max's room was closed so that the twins couldn't go in. When they tried, Max's Dad very gently but firmly told them not to.

Max's Mommy had baked a cake for all of them, and as Max helped Sam into his high chair, Charlotte threw her arms around Max's legs and looked up at her big brother. "I love you, Mash." She grinned at him.

"I love you too, Charlie," Max whispered as he put her into her high chair. And he looked up at his Mommy and Daddy. He loved them all, and he knew they loved him, even if his Mommy and Daddy did get tired and busy once in a while, and the twins kept them hopping . . . and even if the twins did break a toy or take something of his sometimes. That happens in families, but the love between them all was a lot more important. And he was so glad he was home with all of them and not walking around the street alone, the way he had that morning.

"Once when you were little," Mom said, "you decorated our whole bedroom with my lipstick." Max's Mommy laughed as she told him.

"What did you do?" he asked, wide-eyed. "Did you yell at me?"

"No, I wanted to cry because you made a terrible mess of our new bedspread. But I had it cleaned, and the lipstick came out. But the important thing was how much I loved you. I can always get a new bedspread, Max, but there will never be another little boy like you."

"Not even Sam?" He looked over at the twins.

"Not even Sam. You're very special. So is he. So is Charlie." She smiled at all three of them.

Suddenly Max knew that all the little things that had upset him so much didn't really matter. All that mattered was his family and how much he loved them.

That night, as his Daddy tucked him into bed, Max knew how lucky he was. He snuggled into bed with George tucked under his arm. He knew he'd never run away again. He wanted to be here forever. And he drifted off to sleep just after his Mommy and Daddy kissed him.